A House Is a House for Me

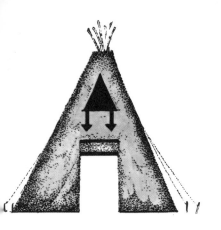     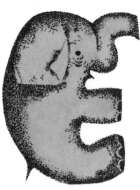

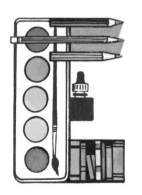

MARY ANN HOBERMAN

Illustrated by BETTY FRASER

PUFFIN BOOKS

To Norman
Builder of my house

Bouquets to Norman

PUFFIN BOOKS
Published by the Penguin Group
Penguin Young Readers Group, 345 Hudson Street, New York, New York 10014, U.S.A.
Penguin Group (Canada), 90 Eglinton Avenue East, Suite 700, Toronto, Ontario, Canada M4P 2Y3
(a division of Pearson Penguin Canada Inc.)
Penguin Books Ltd, 80 Strand, London WC2R 0RL, England
Penguin Ireland, 25 St Stephen's Green, Dublin 2, Ireland (a division of Penguin Books Ltd)
Penguin Group (Australia), 250 Camberwell Road, Camberwell, Victoria 3124, Australia (a division of Pearson Australia Group Pty Ltd)
Penguin Books India Pvt Ltd, 11 Community Centre, Panchsheel Park, New Delhi - 110 017, India
Penguin Group (NZ), 67 Apollo Drive, Mairangi Bay, Auckland 1311, New Zealand (a division of Pearson New Zealand Ltd)
Penguin Books (South Africa) (Pty) Ltd, 24 Sturdee Avenue, Rosebank, Johannesburg 2196, South Africa

Registered Offices: Penguin Books Ltd, 80 Strand, London WC2R 0RL, England

First published in the United States of America by Viking Penguin Inc., a division of Penguin Books USA Inc., 1978
First published by Puffin Books, a division of Penguin Young Readers Group, 1982
This edition published by Puffin Books, a division of Penguin Young Readers Group, 2007

10 9 8

LIBRARY OF CONGRESS CIP DATA IS AVAILABLE.

This Puffin Books edition ISBN 978-0-14-240773-8

Manufactured in China

A hill is a house for an ant, an ant.
A hive is a house for a bee.
A hole is a house for a mole or a mouse

And a house is a house for me!

A web is a house for a spider.

A bird builds its nest in a tree.

There is nothing so snug as a bug in a rug

And a house is a house for me!

A coop? That's a house for a chicken.
A sty? That's a house for a sow.
A fold? That's where sheep all gather to sleep.
A barn? That's a house for a cow.

> (It is also, of course,
> A house for a horse.)

My dog has fleas

A kennel's a house for a dog, a dog.
A dog is a house for a flea.
But when a dog strays, a flea sometimes stays
And then it may move in on me!

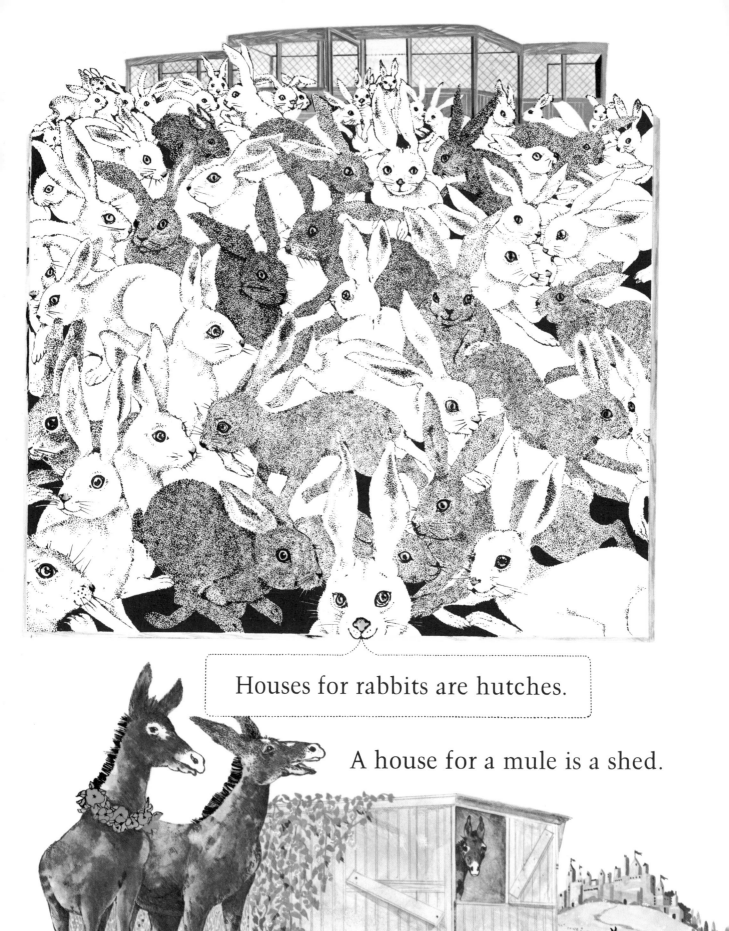

Houses for rabbits are hutches.

A house for a mule is a shed.

A castle's a house for a duchess. A bedbug beds down in a bed.

My House !

A Woman's House is her Castle

CASTLE

HOW TO Build a House

My Castle

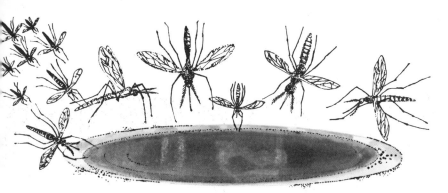

Mosquitoes like mudholes or puddles.

Whales need an ocean or sea.

A fish or a snake may make do with a lake

A shell is a dwelling for shellfish:
For oysters and lobsters and clams.
Each snail has a shell and each turtle as well
But not any lions or lambs.
Lions live out in the open.
Monkeys live up in a tree.
Hippos live down in a river.
Now what do you know about me?

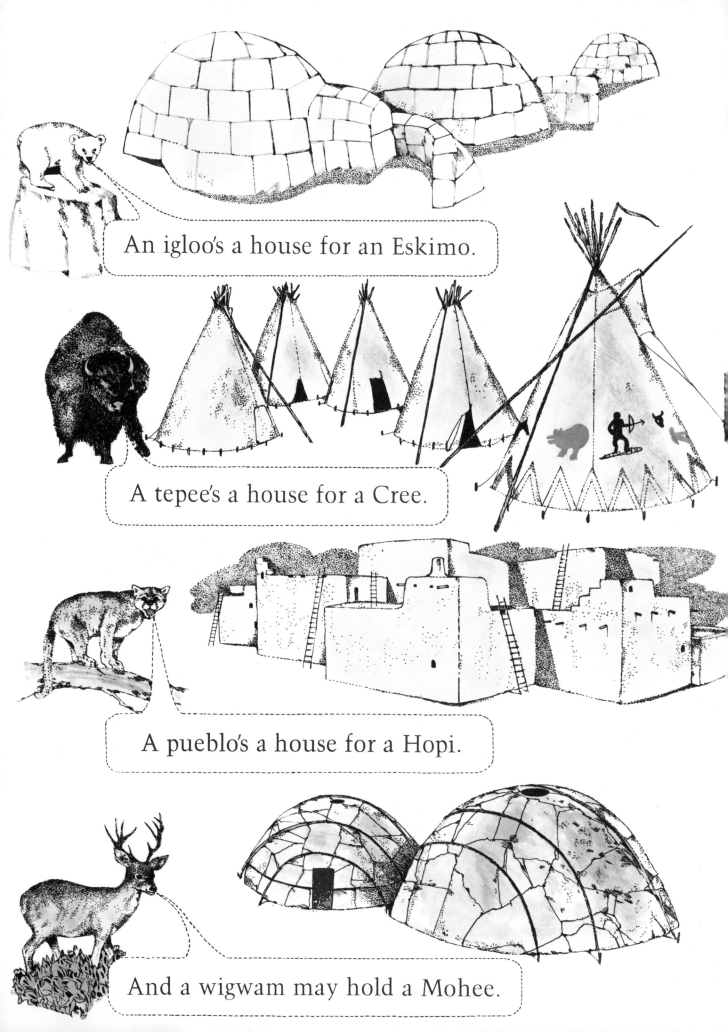

An igloo's a house for an Eskimo.

A tepee's a house for a Cree.

A pueblo's a house for a Hopi.

And a wigwam may hold a Mohee.

A garage is a house for a car or a truck.

A hangar's a house for a plane.

A dock or a slip is a house for a ship

And a terminal's house for a train.

A husk is a house for a corn ear.
A pod is a place for a pea.
A nutshell's a hut for a hickory nut
But what is a shelter for me?

A glove is a house for a hand, a hand.

A stocking's a house for a knee.

A shoe or a boot is a house for a foot

A box is a house for a teabag.
A teapot's a house for some tea.
If you pour me a cup and I drink it all up,
Then the teahouse will turn into me!

Cartons are houses for crackers.
Castles are houses for kings.
The more that I think about houses,
The more things are houses for things.

And if *you* get started in thinking,
I think you will find it is true
That the more that you think about houses for things,
The more things are houses to *you*.

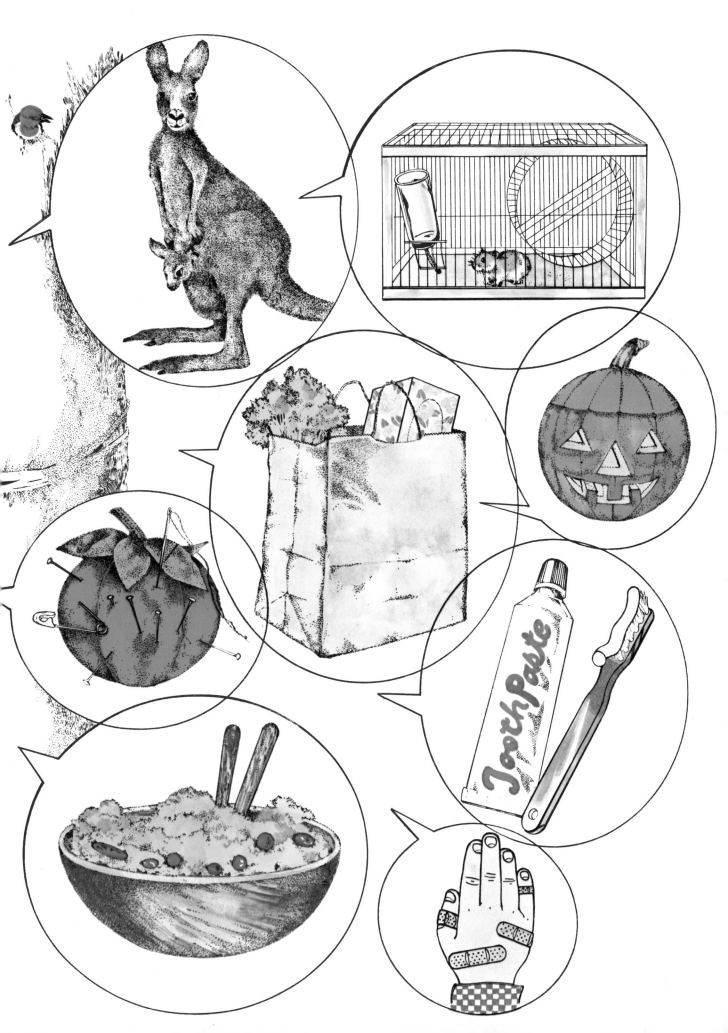

Barrels are houses for pickles
And bottles are houses for jam.
A pot is a spot for potatoes.
A sandwich is home for some ham.

The cookie jar's home to the cookies.

The breadbox is home to the bread.

Perhaps I have started farfetching....
Perhaps I am stretching things some....
A mirror's a house for reflections....
A throat is a house for a hum....
But once you get started in thinking,
You think and you think and you think

How pockets are houses for pennies
And pens can be houses for ink;

How peaches are houses for peachpits
And sometimes are houses for worms;
How trashcans are houses for garbage
And garbage makes houses for germs;

And envelopes, earmuffs and eggshells
And bathrobes and baskets and bins
And ragbags and rubbers and roasters
And tablecloths, toasters and tins…

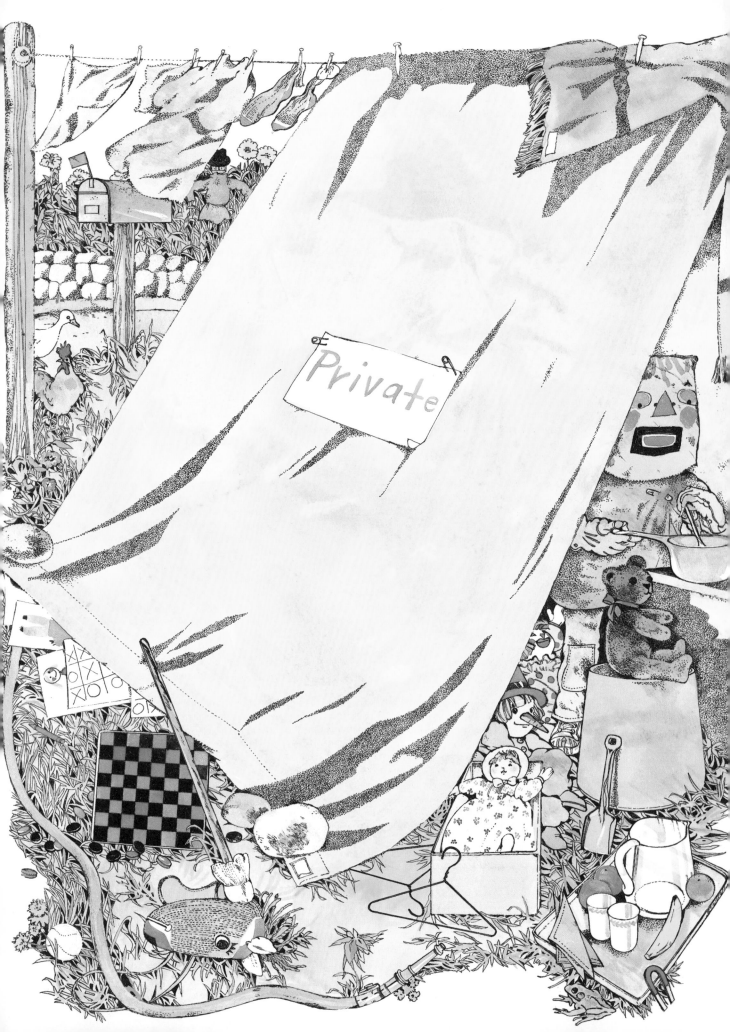

And once you get started in thinking this way,
It seems that whatever you see
Is either a house or it lives in a house,
And a house is a house for me!

A book is a house for a story.
A rose is a house for a smell.

My head is a house for a secret,
A secret I never will tell.

A flower's at home in a garden.
A donkey's at home in a stall.

Each creature that's known has a house of its own

And the earth is a house for us all.